There's a Monster
IN YOUR BOOK

Written by TOM FLETCHER

Illustrated by GREG ABBOTT

Dragonfly Books ——✦—— New York

For Miss Summer Rae, the newest monster in the family! —T.F.

For Roger —G.A.

Copyright © 2017 by Tom Fletcher
Illustrated by Greg Abbott

All rights reserved. Published in the United States by
Dragonfly Books, an imprint of Random House Children's Books,
a division of Penguin Random House LLC, New York.
Originally published in hardcover in the United Kingdom by Puffin Books,
an imprint of Penguin Random House Children's Books, U.K., a division of
Penguin Random House, U.K., London, in 2017. Subsequently published in hardcover
in the United States by Random House Children's Books, a division of
Penguin Random House LLC, New York, in 2017.

Dragonfly Books and colophon are registered trademarks of Penguin Random House LLC.

Visit us on the Web! rhcbooks.com

Educators and librarians, for a variety of teaching tools, visit us at RHTeachersLibrarians.com

The Library of Congress has cataloged the hardcover edition of this work as follows:
Names: Fletcher, Tom, author. | Abbott, Greg, illustrator.
Title: There's a monster in your book / written by Tom Fletcher; illustrated by Greg Abbott.
Other titles: There is a monster in your book
Description: First American edition. | New York: Random House Books for Young Readers, [2017]
Summary: Encourages the reader to shake, tilt, and wiggle the book to remove the little monster inside,
but once it is out, another problem arises.
Identifiers: LCCN 2017001661 (print) | ISBN 978-1-5247-6456-2 (trade) | ISBN 978-0-525-64578-8 (board) |
ISBN 978-1-5247-6457-9 (ebook)
Subjects: | CYAC: Books—Fiction. | Monsters—Fiction. | Humorous stories. | BISAC: JUVENILE FICTION / Humorous Stories. |
JUVENILE FICTION / Interactive Adventures. | JUVENILE FICTION / Imagination & Play.
Classification: LCC PZ7.F6358 The 2017 (print) | DDC [E]—dc23

ISBN 978-0-593-43051-4 (pbk.)

MANUFACTURED IN CHINA   10 9 8 7 6 5 4 3   First Dragonfly Books Edition 2021

Random House Children's Books supports the
First Amendment and celebrates the right to read.

OH NO!
There's a monster in your book!

Let's try to get him out.

shake the book
and turn the page. . . .

Nice try—that knocked him over, but he's
STILL IN YOUR BOOK!

Tickle
his feet and turn the page....

That didn't work—he's just laughing and he's **STILL IN YOUR BOOK!**

Try blowing him away.

BLOOW

really hard and turn the page. . . .

That's better—now he's far away. But he's **STILL IN YOUR BOOK!**

TILT the book to the left. . . .

Now he's over here, but he's

STILL IN YOUR BOOK!

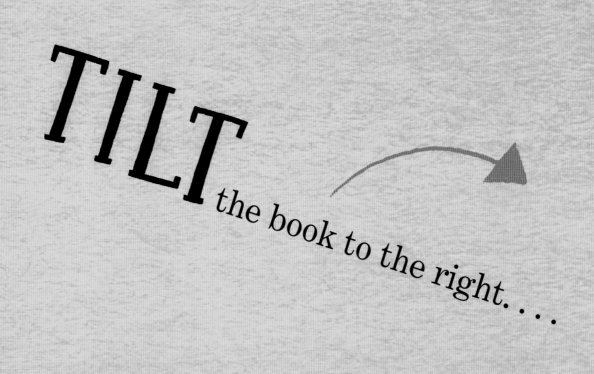

TILT the book to the right. . . .

He's hanging on!

What a naughty little monster!

Give the book a good

Wiggle....

Good, now he's back over there.
But there's **STILL** a monster in your book!

Try **spinning** the book around and around....

Look! He's dizzy!

Quick, make a

LOUD

noise.....

It's working! He's running away!

Make that noise again, but . . .

HE'S GONE!

There **ISN'T** a monster in your book anymore....

Now he's in your room!

Quickly, call him back!
Monster, come back!

Look! Here he is!
He's coming back.

Keep calling him. . . .

Monster!
Come here, little Monster!

PHEW!

He's back in your book.

You don't want a monster loose in your room!
This book is probably the best place to keep him.

Monster, you can stay here in this book!

Pet Monster's head and say good night....

Good night, Monster.

SHHH!
Look! He's fast asleep.

Gently close the book so he doesn't wake up.